FOOTBALL FRAUD

BY JAKE MADDOX

text by

Paul Hoblin

STONE ARCH BOOKS

a capstone imprint

Jake Maddox JV is published by Stone Arch Books, an imprint of Capstone.
1710 Roe Crest Drive
North Mankato, Minnesota 56003
www.capstonepub.com

Library of Congress Cataloging-in-Publication Data
Names: Maddox, Jake, author. | Hoblin, Paul, author.
Title: Football fraud / Jake Maddox; text by Paul Hoblin
Description: North Mankato, Minnesota : Stone Arch Books, [2021] | Series: Jake Maddox JV | Audience: Ages 8–11. | Audience: Grades 4–6. | Summary: "When DeSean Mitchell makes an embarrassing mistake while showboating in the end zone, he ends up costing his football team the game. In the final play, he's tackled and lies on the field in defeat. A teammate assumes he is hurt, and rather than face the shame of his mistake, DeSean fakes an injury. How long will DeSean let the deception go on?"— Provided by publisher. Includes glossary, discussion questions, and writing prompts.
Identifiers: LCCN 2020034815 (print) | LCCN 2020034816 (ebook) | ISBN 9781515882367 (hardcover) | ISBN 9781515883449 (paperback) | ISBN 9781515891963 (pdf)
Subjects: CYAC: Football—Fiction. | Conduct of life—Fiction.
Classification: LCC PZ7.M25643 Foo 2021 (print) | LCC PZ7.M25643 (ebook) | DDC [Fic]—dc23
LC record available at https://lccn.loc.gov/2020034815
LC ebook record available at https://lccn.loc.gov/2020034816

Designer: Dina Her

Image Credits
Shutterstock: Brocreative, design element, David Lee, (ball) Design element, Eky Studio, design element, Isniper, design element, JustPixs, Cover

Printed and bound in the USA. PO 3837

TABLE OF CONTENTS

CHAPTER 1

MR. CLUTCH

DeSean Mitchell stood at his own ten-yard line, waiting for the kickoff. He glanced at the scoreboard.

Home team: 17. Away team: 21.

Seventeen seconds left on the clock.

Moments ago, Park City Middle, the away team, had scored a go-ahead touchdown. Now they were about to kick the ball back to the William H. Johnson Junior High Tigers. The home team. DeSean's team.

Hopefully, they were about to kick the ball to DeSean himself.

Not that kicking it to him would be the smart thing to do.

What Park City should do, DeSean knew, was squib the kick. Keep it low. Get it rolling on the ground. Get someone, anyone, else to pick the ball up and run with it.

Squibbing the kick would take time off the clock. Just as importantly, it would make someone other than DeSean try to beat them.

If he were the coach of the other team, he'd want to keep the ball as far away from him as possible. After all, DeSean was the fastest player at William H. The best player. The best player in the clutch.

Everywhere DeSean looked, he saw teammates who had given up. DeSean didn't blame them. That last touchdown had felt like a punch to the gut.

Park City Middle was their archrival, and for most of the game it had looked like William H. was going to beat them. If they did, they would also win the league.

But then, on fourth and forever, Park City's quarterback had heaved up a prayer—and the prayer had been answered.

His pass was tipped by three or four players and ended up in the tight end's hands as he raced to the end zone.

And now Park City's kicker raised his arm, letting the refs know he was ready. If he did the right thing, in a few seconds some random Tigers player would pick up the bouncing ball. He would stumble a few yards and then get tackled. And the Tigers would still be sixty yards from the end zone with only a few seconds left on the clock.

The refs blew their whistles. The kicker trotted up to the ball on the tee. And then, he did the exact wrong thing.

He reached his leg back and sent it forward, kicking the ball as far as he could. The ball flew past most of William H.'s team, but it didn't fly past DeSean.

As he stood there, waiting for the ball to fall from the sky and into his arms, DeSean thought, *Make them pay for this mistake.*

He trapped the ball against his chest, moved it to the crook of his right elbow, and took off.

Maybe his teammates hadn't given up after all. They were just eighth graders like him, but they'd turned themselves into a wall of blockers. DeSean hurried along the wall until he got almost to the sideline. Then he turned upfield.

There was no one in front of him. No teammates, but no Park City players either.

DeSean turned on the jets. In the spring he was a track star. A sprinter.

And that's what he did now. Sprint.

Down the sideline, past the fifty-yard line, the forty, the thirty.

Out of the corner of his eye, he saw movement.

The kicker.

The last line of Park City's defense.

Make them pay for this mistake, DeSean thought again.

For a split second, he slowed up just a little. It was just enough for the kicker to assume he was going to step out-of-bounds and stop the clock.

The kicker slowed a little too. He had held his hands out so he could push DeSean out-of-bounds, but now he dropped them just slightly.

DeSean planted his left foot and cut across the field. The kicker could only flail at him as he ran by.

He was at the fifteen-yard line now.

The ten.

There was no stopping him. The end zone was right in front of him, and he was about to deliver a game-winning touchdown. It was such an impressive run, the whole school would be talking about it for weeks, maybe even months.

The only thing left to do was celebrate.

At the five-yard line he began high-stepping. Legs straight out, kicking the air.

He thought about how cool he must look as he casually set the ball down while crossing the goal line, still high-stepping.

When he got to the back of the end zone, he tilted his helmet, put his hand next to the ear hole. He was signalling to the crowd and waiting for the cheers to pour through it into his ear.

But there was no cheering. Just shouting.

"The ball! The ball! Get the ball!"

Huh?

DeSean turned around and saw the ball. It was tottering on the grass, where he had left it.

Just outside the goal line.

Had he . . . ? No. He couldn't have. But . . . maybe.

He couldn't believe it.

Yes. He *had.*

The players running toward him, from both teams, confirmed it. He had let go of the ball too early, before he crossed the goal line.

How stupid could I be? DeSean thought.

He sprinted back and dove at the ball. He recovered it just outside the end zone.

Now others were screaming something else: "Time-out!"

* * *

DeSean and his teammates were in a huddle. DeSean kept his eyes aimed at the ground, but he could feel his teammates' glares. He didn't blame them for their anger.

With one second left on the clock, there was just enough time to run one more play.

A play that they shouldn't have needed to run.

"Couldn't you have waited to celebrate until after you scored, DeSean?" one of his teammates asked. "Where was your head, man?"

DeSean didn't have a chance to answer before Coach Drummer arrived.

"Can it," Coach told the other player. "We don't

have time for that kind of comment right now. We need to play now, and we need to play hard. But Mitchell?"

"Yeah, Coach?" DeSean said.

"He's right. Get to the end zone first. Then celebrate," Coach said. "Got it?"

"Yes, Coach," DeSean said softly as he looked down at his feet.

They broke the huddle. Coach jogged back to the sideline.

Mostly, DeSean felt relieved. And determined. He was going to get another chance—a chance to redeem himself. And he was going to do just that.

As DeSean waited for Nick, the Tigers quarterback, to take the snap and hand him the ball, he noticed for the first time that it was cold outside. A chilly breeze swept across the field. There were goose bumps on his arms.

He wondered how long they'd been there. He had been so locked in that he hadn't noticed the weather.

He'd always been able to focus during games. In big moments, he could ignore the weather, the fans. He could focus on what he needed to do.

But now he was noticing other things. The wind wasn't the only thing that was cold. The drop of sweat trickling down his bicep felt icy. His hands felt slippery.

He made them into fists, blew warm breath into them, told himself to refocus.

"Hut!" Nick called, taking the snap.

Nick pivoted to his left and faked the handoff to the fullback. The fake worked. Park City was in their goal-line defense. They had loaded the box to stop a quarterback sneak or a run up the gut.

Nick pitched the ball to DeSean. With the defense collapsed in the middle, all DeSean had to do was run toward the sideline and then cut to the pylon. It should be easy.

When he made it to the edge of his blockers, he saw that once again he had a clear path to the end zone. Without even thinking about it, his legs straightened. He was going to high-step his way across the goal line.

But then he did think about it. He thought about what had happened last time. He thought about his mistake. He thought about what his teammate and Coach had said.

Don't screw this up again, he told himself. *Don't screw it up.*

As he thought this, he saw a Park City linebacker streaking toward him.

The linebacker shouldn't have mattered. He was still a full five yards away, and DeSean was too fast to let him catch him.

But DeSean couldn't run into the end zone because he was currently bobbling the football. Worrying about screwing up—and then seeing that linebacker—broke his focus. DeSean bent his leg again and somehow knocked the ball out of his own hand with his knee.

The bobble didn't last long. But it lasted long enough for the linebacker to close the distance. His helmet and shoulder smacked into DeSean's legs.

DeSean fell to the ground.

He never wanted to get up again.

CHAPTER 2

CHEAP SHOT

The refs blew their whistles and waved their hands. The game was over.

The guy who had tackled DeSean got up. But DeSean didn't. He couldn't.

He couldn't face his teammates.

And that's when he saw one of his teammates leaning over him and peering down.

"You okay?" Nick asked.

"No." DeSean gave an honest answer. He wasn't okay. He'd let his team down—twice. And he didn't think he could ever forgive himself.

"Hey!" Nick shouted, looking up and toward the sideline. "DeSean is hurt! I need some help over here!"

"No . . ." DeSean started to tell his teammate that he wasn't hurt.

But he didn't get to finish the sentence because someone else yelled, "Did you hear that? You injured him!"

As Nick and another teammate pulled him up, DeSean saw two other teammates stomping toward a Park City player. They grabbed his shoulder, spun him around.

It's the linebacker, DeSean realized. *The one who tackled me.*

"That was a totally cheap shot!" his teammate said.

"You speared him!" said the other.

"You led with your helmet!"

"You were trying to injure him!"

They were chest-to-chest with the linebacker. As they screamed at him, their fingers pointed through his face mask.

The refs blew their whistles again. They rushed in and pulled DeSean's teammates away from the linebacker.

DeSean took a step toward these teammates. He needed to tell them it was okay; he was fine. But before he could take another step, Nick said, "Take it easy, man. You don't want to put any weight on your leg."

Nick draped DeSean's arm over his shoulder. Another teammate did the same thing with DeSean's other arm.

DeSean tried one more time to explain that he wasn't injured. But just as he did, everyone started cheering. Fans and players stood and clapped.

DeSean had cost his team the game twice, but everyone was cheering for him.

DeSean closed his mouth. The whistles, the yelling, the cheering—they were too loud for anyone to hear him. Besides, did he want to walk off the field getting booed? Or did he want to limp off the field getting cheered?

The choice was an easy one.

DeSean felt fine, but no one else had to know that. He hopped on one leg as his teammates carried him off the field.

CHAPTER 3

LIMPING AND LYING

"Everything looks good," the doctor said. She pointed at several X-rays of DeSean's knee. "When you described what happened, I was worried you did some serious damage."

"I'm so relieved," DeSean's mom said.

DeSean felt relieved too. But not for the same reason. He was relieved because the doctor hadn't called him a liar in front of his parents.

Lying was exactly what he had been doing ever since he fake limped off the field.

A few hours ago, when the doctor asked him what had happened, he told her the linebacker smashed directly into his knee. He told her he heard a giant *CRACK!* When she asked him to rate his pain between one and ten, he told her, "Nine."

All of these were lies. The linebacker's helmet might have brushed his knee, but it definitely hadn't smashed or cracked it. And he wasn't feeling any pain at all.

DeSean had always been an honest kid. But that first lie—that first limp—had made it easier to tell more lies.

"DeSean," his dad said, "are you paying attention to what the doctor is saying?"

"Sorry," he said. He told himself to stop thinking about his lies and focus.

"It's okay," the doctor said. "I'll say it again. Giving good news is the best part of my job."

She went on to say that she had been worried that he tore the ACL or MCL in his knee. She pointed at the X-rays to show him where his ACL and MCL were located.

"We know a little about the ACL," DeSean's dad said.

"Our daughter tore hers a couple of years ago playing soccer," his mom added.

The doctor nodded. "Well, DeSean's looks great. So does the MCL. In fact, I don't even see much, if any, swelling."

His parents sighed with relief again.

The doctor turned to DeSean. She tilted her head a little. There was an awkward silence. DeSean was sitting on a hospital bed. His leg, the one he claimed he had injured, rested on top of the blanket. When he arrived at the hospital, they had cut his football pants off with scissors. Now his leg felt exposed.

He felt exposed.

The doctor still hadn't said anything. Was she waiting for him to confess? To admit he'd wasted everyone's time? To apologize for being a liar?

She looked at his leg. He looked at it too.

The leg looked normal, of course, and right then DeSean wished it didn't. He wanted it to suddenly swell up to the size of a grapefruit. He even wanted it to start hurting.

Then the doctor couldn't accuse him of lying. Even better, he could stop feeling so bad about lying.

The doctor stepped forward, pressed her fingers into his knee. "Does it hurt more or less when I do this?" she asked.

"The same," he said.

He wasn't lying—not really. His knee didn't hurt when she wasn't doing it, and it didn't hurt now. Technically, his knee really did hurt the same.

"Huh," the doctor said. "I'm stumped."

"Doctor?" his dad asked.

"Usually I wouldn't trust my X-rays as much as I do because of all the swelling right after a knee injury," the doctor replied. "But like I said, there isn't any swelling here, so the pictures are really clear. There's no structural damage to the knee. I'm surprised he's feeling this much pain."

"Any guesses?" DeSean's mom asked.

"Sometimes the brain can tell us there's pain even when structurally there shouldn't be," the doctor said. "My recommendation is that DeSean takes it easy the next few days. I'm guessing the pain will go away on its own. If not, bring him back."

"Does that mean he can't play football?" his mom asked.

"Honestly? It's up to you," the doctor said, looking at DeSean. "I don't like hearing about that pain, so by all means, take a few days off. But you're not at any greater risk of injuring the leg than anyone else, so it's up to you when you return to the field."

CHAPTER 4

MR. CRUTCH

Never.

That's when DeSean wanted to return to the field.

Not ever again.

How could he go back? His knee may not have been injured, but his confidence was.

He had always thought of himself as Mr. Clutch. The best player for the biggest moment. But now? After screwing everything up—twice? He wasn't sure he even deserved to play anymore. His belief in himself was as shredded as his football pants.

Speaking of the pants, they were lying in a pile on his bed. DeSean knew he should toss them aside, crawl under the covers, try to get some sleep. But he couldn't. If he fell asleep, he'd skip right to morning.

He desperately wanted to slow down time. When morning came, he would no longer be able to hide alone in his room. He'd have to go to school. And he'd have to return those cut-up pants.

"Sorry about the shredded pants, Coach. When you go in for a knee injury, they cut off your pants," he'd have to say. "So they were destroyed while I faked an injury because I was embarrassed."

If anything, he was even more embarrassed now. Everyone at school would take one look at him walking just fine and know.

They would know he'd been faking his injury. He didn't deserve their concern. He deserved their laughter. He'd lost the game for his team. There was no denying the loss was his fault. And then he had the nerve to lie about being hurt on top of it.

But just because he deserved their laughter and their angry glares didn't mean he wanted to experience them.

So instead of going to sleep, he crept out of his bedroom. As silently as he could, he crept down the hall. It was late, and he didn't want to wake his parents.

As far as they were concerned, DeSean was still in pain. They were worried that he would want to rush back onto the field, and they had made a special effort to talk to him about playing football again too quickly.

"We know you have a big game coming up," his dad had said when they got home from the hospital. "But you can take a day or two off."

His mom had agreed. "Your teammates will understand. So will your coach."

"Okay?" they'd both asked.

"Will you promise to skip practice tomorrow and maybe the next day?" his mom added.

DeSean had nodded his head.

He could definitely skip a couple of practices. In fact, if his plan worked, he was going to skip the rest of the season.

He tiptoed down the hall and nudged open his older sister's bedroom door. The door creaked a little. It hadn't been used in a long time. His sister had left for college a couple of months ago, and as far as DeSean knew, no one had entered since.

He didn't dare close the door behind him because he didn't want it to creak again.

Using the flashlight on his phone, DeSean moved toward the closet. Unlike the other door, this one swung open soundlessly. DeSean didn't know where exactly to look, but he knew what he was looking for.

Luckily, the closet was small, so it didn't take long.

He spotted the crutches first. They leaned against the corner of the closet. And the other thing he was looking for was there too. It was dark and he could barely see it, even with his phone flashlight. But he knew what it was—a leg brace.

His sister had used both the brace and the crutches after she tore her ACL. Her injury was years ago. She didn't need this stuff anymore. So DeSean figured he'd use it instead.

CHAPTER 5

FRIENDLY ADVICE

"What was that?" Alejandro asked.

Alejandro was DeSean's best friend. He was also DeSean's daily ride to school. Alejandro was a year older in school, but two years older in age. He had flunked ninth grade last year and had to repeat the year. He was the only kid at William H. Johnson Junior High who had a car because he was the only one who had a license.

DeSean opened the door to Alejandro's truck. He was about to explain that the rattling sound was his crutches. He'd tossed the crutches into the bed of the truck.

"And what's that?" Alejandro asked, watching as DeSean strapped the brace around his knee.

"A knee brace," DeSean answered.

He said the words under his breath. Windows were open all over his house, and he didn't want his parents to hear. If they did, they'd be as confused as Alejandro.

He hopped into the front seat, slammed the door shut, and rolled up the window.

"I can see that it's a knee brace, D," Alejandro said, shaking his head. "But why are you wearing it? Based on how quickly you jumped in, it doesn't look like you need it."

"It's a long story," DeSean said.

"You've got about four minutes to tell it," Alejandro said. Four minutes was how long driving to school took.

"Promise to keep a secret?" DeSean asked.

Alejandro didn't answer, but he didn't have to. Of course, he promised. Keeping promises were what best friends were for.

DeSean told him everything. Dropping the ball too early on the kick return. Bobbling it and letting himself get tackled on the last play of the game. Feeling too ashamed to get up, and everyone thinking he must be injured.

"So that's what I'm going to be," DeSean said.

"What?" asked Alejandro.

"Injured," DeSean said.

They were pulling into the school parking lot.

"Sorry, D. That doesn't sound like the best idea I've ever heard," Alejandro said.

"You got a better one?" DeSean asked.

"Come clean? Face the music? Tell the truth?" Alejandro shook his head.

"No way, man. There's no way I can admit that to everyone. Do you know what people would say? How they would react?" DeSean said.

Alejandro backed into a parking spot and shifted the truck into park. He looked at DeSean. "So play this out for me."

"What?" DeSean asked.

"The plan," Alejandro said. "You're going to try to trick everyone into thinking you're injured until . . . when?"

"Next week," DeSean said. "After our last game of the season. It's a rematch against Park City. Winner wins the league."

"Sounds like they could use you," Alejandro said.

"Why? So I can screw up again? I'm sure Grant can at least hold on to the football." Grant was the backup running back. "Besides, since when did you care so much about football?"

Alejandro said, "I'm just trying to figure out—"

"The plan," DeSean interrupted. "You told me."

What's gotten into me? DeSean wondered. *Why am I angry all of a sudden?*

Then he realized the reason for his anger: He felt

guilty. He wasn't angry at Alejandro. He was angry at himself. He was doing all this just because he wasn't brave enough to fess up like Alejandro said he should.

"Can I ask one more question?" Alejandro asked.

"What?" DeSean said.

"Aren't knee injuries that make you wear one of those"—he pointed at the brace—"supposed to last longer than a week?"

It was a good point. How long could he keep pretending? His parents didn't know he was pretending at all—was he really going to keep lying to them day after day, week after week?

"Like I said," Alejandro said, turning off the ignition, "this doesn't sound like one of your best ideas."

DeSean watched his best friend open the door and walk around the truck. In the rearview mirror, DeSean saw Alejandro reach into the bed of his truck and grab the crutches. When DeSean opened his door, Alejandro handed him the crutches.

"Let's get one thing straight, D. Just because I'm going to walk with you into school doesn't mean I support your plan," Alejandro said. "It just means I'm still your friend. And if people figure out you're faking, you're going to need a friend."

CHAPTER 6

WARNING BELL

"After you," Alejandro said.

He held open the front door of the school. DeSean hopped on one leg and swung himself forward with his crutches.

Crossing the parking lot had taken a long time. After all, DeSean had never used crutches before.

Alejandro and DeSean were the last two students to enter the building. The five-minute bell had already rung. Everywhere, students scrambled to get what they needed from their lockers before the school day started.

"I have to get going," Alejandro said. "You going to be okay?"

DeSean nodded. He knew how important school was to Alejandro. Ever since he found out he had to repeat ninth grade, he'd faced up to his mistakes and made sure he didn't fail his classes again.

Besides, DeSean wasn't really injured. Alejandro was being really nice walking with him and holding the door for him. But doing these things really wasn't necessary. The extra attention actually made DeSean feel even more guilty.

Alejandro turned to go to his first class, but he didn't make it far. He couldn't get around the crowd of people heading their way.

"Whoah! Dude!" Nick called. He was surrounded by what looked to be most of the team. There must have been thirty, even forty of his teammates moving together.

And they were all looking at DeSean—at DeSean's knee, more specifically.

"That thing looks heavy-duty," Nick said, pointing at the brace. "What did the doctor say?"

DeSean mumbled something about his ACL. He mumbled for two reasons. First, telling a lie under his breath was easier than saying it loudly. Second, he was distracted.

Why was the whole team standing in a group?

Sure, they were teammates. They liked each other. Many of them sat next to each other at lunch.

But right now? With only minutes to go before class started?

"I guess Royce is right," Nick said.

"Of course I'm right." Royce Anderson stepped out from behind a group of linemen.

Royce was a short, skinny eighth grader. But in some ways, he was the most powerful kid in school. His power came from being the most active reporter for the *Billy Beacon*, the school's online newspaper. Students read and talked about his articles in the halls, during lunch, before and after classes.

And students weren't the only ones who cared about what Royce reported; the adults read his articles too. If you wanted more funding, the best way to get the principal's attention was to ask Royce to write a nice article about your sport or club.

"Right about what?" DeSean asked.

"Suspending Jimmy Harrison," Nick said.

"Who?" DeSean asked.

"The linebacker who ended your football career," Royce said.

"My career?" This was all too weird to make much sense to DeSean.

"You said it yourself," Royce said. "He took out your ACL. A lot of athletes never truly come back from that injury."

This was true. His sister had been on track to be a Division I soccer player. After her knee injury, several scholarship offers went away. Luckily, a few schools still wanted her to play for them. But she told DeSean this summer that her knee still didn't feel quite right.

"But—" he started to say. What he wanted to say was, *I didn't tear my ACL.*

Instead, he was interrupted by Royce: "There's no excuse for a tackle like that. His cheap shot is why I got the whole team together. I'm going to write an article demanding that Jimmy Harrison be suspended. And I'm going to say the whole team agrees."

DeSean looked at all his teammates. They nodded. They put their fists in the air.

"We got your back," someone said.

More nods.

"But . . . ," DeSean said again.

The one-minute bell rang.

Before they dispersed for class, his teammates clapped DeSean's shoulder and back. Random students clapped his back too. They shouted encouraging words at him.

Thirty seconds later, there were only three students left in the hallway—DeSean, Royce . . . and Alejandro.

DeSean had forgotten his best friend was still there. "Don't you need to get to class?" he asked.

"I haven't been late once this year," Alejandro said. "If I'm late, I'll just tell my teacher the truth. I was helping a friend."

"I can help him get to class," Royce said.

But Alejandro didn't move. "That's not what I meant," he said.

DeSean knew it wasn't. Alejandro wasn't trying to help him get to class. He was trying to help him tell the truth. He wanted DeSean to come clean here and now—to tell the truth about his fake injury.

DeSean opened his mouth to just fess up. But all that came out was: "I mean, getting a player suspended? Doesn't suspending him seem a little harsh?"

"Harsh?" Royce said. "He might have ended your career! the least he can do is miss one game."

"He didn't . . . ," DeSean said. He was looking at both Alejandro and Royce as they waited for him to finish. He knew he should finish the sentence, but he also knew Royce was a reporter. If he told him the real story, it would become just that: a story in the *Billy Beacon*. Everyone would read about all his lies.

The start-of-class bell rang. Alejandro shook his head and headed for class.

"C'mon," Royce said. "I'll walk you to first period. I'll just tell your teacher you were working on a story with me. I use that excuse all the time."

CHAPTER 7

BACKUP

DeSean had made it through the school day. He'd crutched from one class to another as everyone watched him, pity in their eyes. Everyone was so nice to him. They moved out of his way. They put reassuring hands on his shoulder. They offered to carry his books for him.

Knowing that everyone could be so nice felt good. But their kindness also felt horrible.

He hadn't done a single good thing since he dropped the football on the one-yard line. He knew he hadn't, even if they didn't. And getting rewarded for doing bad things felt awful.

Now that the school day was over, he could finally get away from students and their sympathy. Well, almost.

He still needed to go to practice. Not to play, of course. But when players were injured, Coach still expected them to show up for practice. They'd made a commitment to the team, he said. That commitment didn't go away.

So DeSean stood on the sideline and watched his teammates run through plays. What he saw didn't look good.

Grant Melvin, the backup running back, was a backup running back for a reason. Saying that wasn't mean; it was just the truth.

He wasn't as fast as DeSean or as strong or as nimble.

But the worst part was that he didn't know the plays. Like, at all.

After Grant ran to the wrong hole for the third time, Coach Drummer angrily blew his whistle and told everyone to take a water break. All the players shuffled off the field.

Except for Grant.

Coach made him stay. DeSean watched Coach try again to explain the plays to Grant. He watched Grant nod his head but his face was filled with uncertainty. He was wearing a helmet, but even through his face mask, his eyes looked big and wet. DeSean was pretty sure he was about to cry.

Coach must have thought so too, because he lowered his voice, smiled, and tapped Grant on the head. "Don't worry, Melvin," he said. "We've got a week to figure this out. Go grab some water."

Relieved, Grant hustled away.

DeSean was pretty sure Grant was running faster now than he had while practicing. Clearly, he wanted to get off the field as quickly as possible.

Unlike DeSean, though, he wasn't going to be

able to stay off the field for long. His teammates were already jogging back to run more plays.

And they'd need a running back to do it.

If DeSean wasn't there, someone had to be.

Grant had gotten some water, but unlike the others, he didn't jog back. He walked. DeSean could see the fear in his eyes. Was it fear of getting hit? Or fear of screwing up?

Here was something else DeSean could add to his List of Things I Feel Guilty About: putting Grant in this situation.

He didn't know Grant very well. But he was pretty sure Grant didn't even want to be on the team. This was the first year he'd played football. And he joined the team a week late. Everyone knew why. Some jerk had beaten him up.

The next day, he'd wandered into Coach's office with his dad while the team was in the locker room putting on their pads. Grant had stood there while his dad did all the talking. His dad said he wanted to toughen up his son. Coach had said that's not really what football was for, but his dad wouldn't take no for an answer. His son was joining—that was that.

DeSean was pretty sure Grant decided to play running back because he knew DeSean was a star. He figured he wouldn't have to play much or at all.

DeSean was also pretty sure Coach let Grant play running back for the same reason. Coach knew Grant didn't want to play, so he had DeSean take all the snaps in practice and in games.

Until now.

DeSean was thinking about the mess he'd made when someone yelled, "DeSean, watch out!"

Out of the corner of his eye, DeSean saw a football tumble out of the sky. Then he saw two players tumbling after it. Without thinking, he jumped out of the way.

He landed on both feet and stood there, looking at the two players as they picked themselves up.

"You okay?" someone asked.

"You good?" someone else said.

"Mitchell?"

His teammates weren't questioning the two players. They were questioning him.

And only one person called him by his last name.

DeSean looked toward the field. All the players stared at him. So did Coach.

"Mitchell?" Coach said again. The worry in everybody's face matched the worry in Coach's voice.

Because of my knee, he finally realized.

His crutches were gone. He must have thrown them aside when he jumped out of the way.

For all they knew, a teammate with a bad knee injury had just jumped and landed with full force on that very same knee.

How had Alejandro put it? He had said DeSean should "come clean." If there was ever a time to tell the truth, the time was right now.

He might not even need to say much. Pretty soon his team would realize that he must not be injured.

All he had to do was stand there and let them figure it out.

Instead, he fell over and shouted out in pain.

"Here," one of his teammates said.

DeSean looked up. The two teammates who had tumbled toward him were now standing over him. They held out his crutches.

"Sorry," one of them said. His voice was shaky. Clearly, he meant it.

Me too, DeSean thought.

CHAPTER 8

LYING AND FLYING

DeSean was surprised to see Alejandro sitting in his truck in the parking lot. He had figured he'd have to take the late bus home.

It was normal for Alejandro to stay late after school. He stayed late every day. While DeSean was practicing, Alejandro met with his teachers and worked on his homework.

It was also normal for Alejandro to give him a ride home. Since they usually finished up at the same time, it was no trouble for Alejandro to give DeSean a lift.

But today DeSean was later than usual. Coach Drummer had kept him after practice to ask him over and over again if he was okay. He'd suggested they call the doctor and tell her what happened.

"Just in case you damaged the knee any further," Coach had said. When DeSean had said he was fine for the twentieth time, Coach finally let up.

"Promise me you'll tell your parents all about what happened—okay, Mitchell?" he said. DeSean had nodded his head. At this point, lying was becoming natural to him.

Lastly, Coach had told him he'd decided to change his policy. "You don't need to come to practice anymore, Mitchell. Season's almost over. Your health is more important than being with your team for a few days."

Finally, some good news. If he didn't have to go to practice, he wouldn't. The farther he could get from the gridiron, the easier it'd be to distract himself from his gridiron guilt.

And now some more good news. Alejandro had waited for him. He knew his best friend was disappointed in him, but he'd still waited.

DeSean had only been pretending to need crutches for one day, but he was already sick of it. His armpits hurt. And he hated having Alejandro watch him hop across the parking lot.

It was late. The parking lot was mostly empty. Maybe he could stop using the crutches and just walk across the lot. Even better, maybe he could sprint. He had forgotten how much he loved to run. Getting to run was why he loved football. It was why he was on the track team in the spring.

Legs and arms pumping, flying from one place to another. It was an amazing feeling.

DeSean stopped. He looked at Alejandro. He smiled. He tucked the crutches under his arms like they were long footballs. Alejandro's truck was still a good forty yards away. And DeSean was going to sprint every yard of it.

SCREECH!

A white Lexus pulled up next to him.

"Hey, DeSean," a kid's voice said.

DeSean looked at the driver. She was an adult. And she had her window up.

"Hey," the voice said.

DeSean turned to where he realized the voice was coming from—the back seat. "Oh. Hey, Royce. Do you have a driver? Like, someone who drives you around?"

Royce had been smiling, but now he frowned, confused. "You mean my mom?"

His answer made sense. Except . . . "Why aren't you in the front seat?" DeSean asked. "You sit in the back when it's just the two of you?"

"I don't know, man. Who cares?" Royce's smile returned. "I have good news!"

DeSean waited for him to share the good news.

"People read my article about suspending Jimmy Harrison," Royce said.

"Don't people read all of your articles?" DeSean asked.

"I don't mean people as in students or teachers," Royce said. "I mean important people."

DeSean didn't understand. "Like . . . ?"

"Like the people who run the football conference," Royce said as he leaned toward the window. "They're having a meeting tomorrow night to discuss whether to let Jimmy play next week. Word is, Jimmy has been asked to attend the meeting."

DeSean looked away to make sure Alejandro was still there. He was. And he was watching. "Seriously, Royce. I really don't think you need to do this."

Royce's smile faded again. But just for a moment. "*I'm* not doing this. *We're* doing this. All of us. I'm going to get the whole team to show up and protest." Royce leaned out of his car window. "You're doing this, DeSean."

"What do you mean?" DeSean asked.

"I mean this will be way more effective if you give

your side of what happened," Royce said. "Fair is fair. They're going to let Jimmy give his side, so they need to hear from you too."

DeSean's brain was spinning. He needed to think of something to say so he wouldn't have to speak at the meeting. "You know my side. He didn't hurt me, so he—"

"Wait—what?" Royce's smile had completely vanished now. He leaned out of the window further, squinting his eyes.

Was he just noticing now that DeSean was carrying the crutches instead of using them?

Royce's eyes opened. Like he'd figured something out. Like he had a lead on a new story.

A new scandal.

DeSean put the ends of the crutches down on the parking lot. He pretended to wince in pain as he lifted his "bad" leg and put all his weight on his "good" leg.

"I mean," DeSean said, "he didn't try to hurt me, so let's just let it go."

Royce leaned back into the car. "What do you mean he didn't try to hurt you? He dove at your legs, helmet first. What did he think was going to happen?"

"I just don't think I can do it," DeSean said.

"You'd be doing him a favor," Royce said.

"A favor?" DeSean asked.

"I just talked with a bunch of your teammates," Royce said. "They're saying that if Jimmy does get to play, they'll have to take matters into their own hands."

Matters into their own hands? DeSean thought. *Seriously?*

"They would seriously hurt another player?" DeSean was talking to himself as much as Royce, but Royce answered anyway.

"They'd be hurting him for you. It's called being a good teammate. This is your chance to be a good teammate too. Think of it this way: If you don't speak tomorrow night, you could be putting not only Jimmy at risk, but all your teammates."

DeSean waited for him to finish his thought.

"Someone who is willing to tackle like that once," Royce said, "is probably willing to do it again. Especially if there are no consequences after he does it the first time."

DeSean didn't know what to say, which was fine by Royce. He must have already decided the conversation was over because he was rolling up his window.

"See you tomorrow night," he said as the window closed.

His chauffeur—er, his mom—drove him away.

DeSean made a slow, pathetic, fake-injured, crutching walk to Alejandro's truck. When he got there, Alejandro asked, "So, what was that all about, DeSean?"

He took DeSean's crutches and heaved them into the bed while DeSean relayed the conversation.

"You going to go through with it?" Alejandro asked as he drove out of the parking lot.

DeSean didn't answer.

"Sounds like you're going to have to do something," Alejandro said. "If Royce expects you to, he'll make sure everyone else does too."

DeSean mumbled an answer.

"Huh?" Alejandro asked. "What did you say, D?"

"I said I don't know," DeSean admitted. "Okay? I don't even know what the right thing to do is."

"Bull, D," Alejandro said. "You do know what the right thing is. This kid didn't do anything. You're going to let him get punished anyway?"

"Maybe he did do something," DeSean said.

Alejandro took his hand off the wheel and backhand-slapped DeSean's brace. "That hurt me more than it hurt you," he said, shaking his hand.

"I'm not saying he hurt me," DeSean said. "I'm saying he could have hurt me. I mean, that was a pretty stupid way to tackle someone, right? Like, you shouldn't tackle with your helmet. We're all taught that. And you definitely shouldn't dive into someone's knee with your helmet. If he gets suspended, he'll deserve it, won't he?"

"Is that what Royce told you?" asked Alejandro.

DeSean didn't answer his question, but he tried out another one of Royce's points. "Besides, my teammates are talking about taking matters into their own hands if Jimmy doesn't get suspended. If I don't speak up tomorrow, he might get really hurt."

"Wait. Are you trying to claim you'd be helping Jimmy?" asked Alejandro. "Is that seriously what you think you're doing?"

"I'm just saying he shouldn't have tackled me helmet first, and someone's got to speak up to make sure it doesn't happen again," DeSean replied.

They were idling in front of DeSean's house.

Alejandro sighed. "You're right, D."

DeSean was surprised. "Really?"

"Someone's got to speak up," Alejandro said.

DeSean sat there silently a few seconds, trying to figure out what Alejandro meant.

"You can leave your crutches if you want," he said, pointing his thumb behind them. He tapped DeSean's brace with a knuckle. "This too. That way, you won't have to sneak them in and out of your house."

CHAPTER 9

SOFT KNOCKS

"DeSean. DESEAN." DeSean's mom's voice was loud and clear.

"Hmmm. What?" DeSean said.

He was sitting at breakfast with his mom and dad, but he was zoned out in his own world.

"You seem distracted," his dad said, taking a sip of coffee. "Why do you keep looking out the window?"

"No reason," said DeSean. "I'm looking for Alejandro. He's like five minutes late."

Five minutes may not have sounded like much to his mom and dad, but Alejandro was never late.

"Are you worried about being late?" his mom asked, looking up from her eggs. "Want a ride?"

"No, I'm not worried about being late," he said. But he kept looking out the window.

This was true. Being late to school didn't worry him. What scared him was why Alejandro would be late picking him up.

DeSean had hardly slept last night. The more he thought about his conversation with Alejandro, the more Alejandro's words freaked him out. "Someone's got to speak up," he'd said. And DeSean was pretty sure the someone Alejandro was referring to was Alejandro himself.

But what did he mean by "speak up"? Speak up to whom? Alejandro wouldn't snitch on him . . . would he?

DeSean heard keys jingling.

"I'll take him," his dad said.

"What? . . . No. Really," DeSean said. "I'm sure he'll be here any minute."

Maybe that's why Alejandro volunteered to keep his crutches and brace in the truck. By not showing up this morning, maybe he was trying to force DeSean to come clean to his parents and then the school. He couldn't keep pretending to have an injured knee if he didn't have a knee brace.

"Is there some reason you don't want your dear old dad to drop you off?" his dad asked.

His mom laughed. "I guess we're not cool enough," she said.

His dad twirled his keys around his finger and put them in his pocket like he was a cowboy holstering his pistol. "Who's not cool now?" he said.

His mom laughed again. "UGH. YOU aren't. If I were him, I wouldn't want a ride from you either."

DeSean turned most of his attention to his weirdo parents. They were both smiling at him. They were also both completely not cool. But he didn't mind their lack of coolness. He just didn't want to let them down. What if he had to tell them about all his lying?

Or, worse, what if he had to tell them about all the lying and they still made him go to school and tell everyone else too?

He needed those crutches. He needed that brace. There was no way he could go to school without them.

His dad took the keys out of his pocket, spun them on his finger, and used them to point out the window.

"Looks like I won't get to embarrass you today," he said.

DeSean saw that his dad was right. Alejandro was there, idling on the curb like always. Thank goodness.

There was a knock on the door.

Huh?

This made no sense. Alejandro never got out of his truck in the morning, and he hadn't gotten out this morning. DeSean could see him clearly through the window, sitting in his truck, hands on the steering wheel.

Another knock—soft but clear.

Who could it be?

DeSean opened the door. A kid stood there, about DeSean's height but bulkier. His muscular arms hung uncomfortably at his sides. DeSean thought he recognized him, but from where?

"DeSean?" the boy asked, his voice as soft and clear as the knock on the door.

"Yeah?" DeSean said.

"I'm Jimmy," he said. "Jimmy Harrison. And I've come here to say 'I'm sorry.'"

DeSean's parents were still in the kitchen, but they were looking at DeSean with tilted heads. The head tilts were their way of saying, "Everything okay?"

He nodded at them. "I'll be right outside, okay?"

The two boys sat down next to each other on the front stoop, which was a mistake. Jimmy really did have wide shoulders. The stoop was just barely big enough to fit both Jimmy and DeSean.

DeSean's shoulder was pressed against the railing.

Being so close actually made it harder to see each other because they couldn't twist their bodies enough to make eye contact.

Come to think of it, DeSean thought, *maybe this is the perfect spot to have this conversation.*

Neither one of them wanted to look at the other. Sitting side by side made it easier for them to both stare at their feet as they talked.

"I'm sorry," Jimmy said again.

"Did Alejandro bring you here?" DeSean asked.

He was pretty sure Jimmy nodded.

"How'd he find you?" DeSean asked.

"He found me online," Jimmy said.

DeSean looked up at Alejandro's truck. He was still there, looking straight ahead through the windshield as though he was driving rather than parked.

"What did he tell you?" DeSean asked.

"Enough," Jimmy said. "Enough to get me to come here."

DeSean wasn't sure what that meant. He wasn't sure there was anything Alejandro could have said to get him to go to Jimmy's house and apologize.

"I'm sorry," Jimmy said for the third time.

"You keep saying that," DeSean said, "but I don't understand what you're apologizing for. You know I'm not hurt, right?"

Another shoulder jolt.

"I'm sorry for the way I tackled you," Jimmy said. "I would never, ever do that on purpose."

"But you did do it," DeSean said.

"Not on purpose," Jimmy repeated.

"I don't understand." DeSean heard Jimmy sigh. He felt his shoulder slump.

"I tripped," Jimmy said.

"Over what?" DeSean asked.

"Over nothing," Jimmy replied. "I was running across the field, and I saw you, and I tried to speed up. The next thing I knew, I was falling. I thought for sure I'd cost us the game. But then there your feet and legs were. I tried to lift my head up and use my arms and shoulder but it was too late."

DeSean didn't get it. Why was Jimmy telling this story like it was some deep, dark confession?

"So why do you keep saying 'Sorry'?" DeSean asked. "You didn't do anything wrong. Everybody falls."

"I lied," Jimmy said. "To my teammates. Or at least I didn't tell them the truth. After I tackled you, honestly, I was embarrassed. But then my teammates swarmed me. They lifted me up. They knocked helmets with me. I was the hero of the game. It wasn't until your teammates started yelling at me that I even thought about you. I saw you lying there, and I watched them carry you off the field, and I didn't say 'Sorry.' I knew they were going to take you to the hospital, but I didn't even clap as you hopped off the field."

DeSean couldn't believe what he was hearing. "But I was the one who was lying," he said.

This was crazy. Why was this kid doing the apologizing? If anything, Jimmy's apology just made DeSean feel worse. Jimmy was beating himself up for not checking on a player from the other team. DeSean had allowed his whole school to try to get revenge against Jimmy.

"I didn't know that," Jimmy said. "I thought you were really hurt. And then I did my best not to think about you one way or the other. I was actually mad when my parents asked about you and suggested I come visit you—not because it was a bad idea, but because thinking about you made me feel guilty."

DeSean knew all about feeling guilty.

"I just wanted to keep being the hero," Jimmy said. "Even when I found out I might get suspended, I wasn't going to tell the conference committee the truth. I was going to let them suspend me if they needed to, just so I didn't have to admit out loud that my tackle was pure dumb luck."

There was a long silence between them. Finally,

DeSean said, "And Alejandro convinced you to come over here and admit all of that?"

He said the words loudly enough that he was pretty sure Alejandro could hear. Alejandro didn't look away from the windshield, but he smiled.

"He's good at making a person feel guilty, isn't he?" DeSean said to Jimmy and Alejandro.

Jimmy laughed. "He's a master at it," he said, also loudly enough for Alejandro to hear.

Jimmy stood up, walked down a few steps, and faced DeSean.

"I'm sorry," he said for the fifth time.

He put out his hand. DeSean was pretty sure he was supposed to shake the hand, but he didn't. He clasped Jimmy's hand in his own and used it to pull himself up.

He looked Jimmy in the eye. "I'm sorry too."

But he knew that saying sorry wasn't enough. He needed to make this right.

In public.

For all to see.

"Hey, Alejandro," DeSean said over Jimmy's shoulder.

Alejandro took his eyes off the windshield. "Yeah?"

"Could you give both of us a ride to the meeting tonight?"

CHAPTER 10

SORE LOSERS

"What have I done?" DeSean asked.

The three of them were in the truck. Alejandro, DeSean, Jimmy. Shoulder to shoulder to shoulder.

The truck idled in the community education parking lot. The community-ed building was where the football conference committee meeting was taking place. And the sidewalk in front of the building was filled with people protesting.

The three boys stared at the protestors for a moment from behind the truck's windshield. Many of the protestors were DeSean's teammates, but a lot of them were just his classmates.

"Su-u-spend him!" they chanted. They held up signs that said the same thing.

"It's not just you," Jimmy said. "I did this too."

Sure enough, DeSean's teammates and classmates were chanting at Jimmy's teammates and classmates. And vice versa.

"So-ore losers!" they chanted back.

They'd arrived just in time, from the looks of it.

"We better get out there before a fight breaks out," Jimmy said.

"You need me?" Alejandro asked.

"Only if we need to separate them," DeSean said.

"I'll keep an eye out, D," Alejandro said.

"Thanks," DeSean said.

As DeSean and Jimmy walked together across the parking lot, their schoolmates saw them coming.

"DeSean! I was worried you weren't going to make it!" someone from William H. Johnson said.

"Jimmy," someone from Park City said, "we got your back!"

The two groups seemed confused at first.

That's Jimmy? DeSean's side must have been thinking.

DeSean's the guy walking next to him? Jimmy's side seemed to wonder.

Football was strange that way. Thanks to helmets and face masks and pads, you decide the other team's players are your enemies and never even know what they look like.

The two sides were too stunned to keep fighting. They parted like a sea as DeSean and Jimmy walked through them on their way to the meeting. DeSean wondered how many of them wanted to know what had happened to his crutches.

Jimmy opened the door. Before they entered, DeSean turned to the two sides. "Anyone who wants to hear the full story should come inside with us. But it's pretty simple."

"I tripped," Jimmy said.

"And I lied." DeSean gestured to his knee, just in case anyone had failed to notice he wasn't wearing a brace.

CHAPTER 11

END ZONE

DeSean stood on the sideline, scratching his leg. He was surrounded by thirty of his teammates. But he felt alone.

He'd been standing in this exact spot for most of the first half, and not a single teammate had said a word to him. Not that he blamed them. If he were them, he wouldn't want anything to do with himself either.

He couldn't believe he was even allowed to stay on the team. No, *allowed* was the wrong word. He was forced to stay on the team, by his parents and Coach Drummer.

Big, dramatic speeches in front of his teammates and classmates took some courage, they said. Especially when your school had Royce Anderson of the *Billy Beacon* making sure every single student in the school heard about what you did.

DeSean had spent the last few days walking by students in the halls who were looking at their phones and then pointing at him. If they weren't staring or pointing, they were bumping into him or even tripping him, asking if he needed his crutches again.

But the real courage, they said, was getting back up—was showing up at all—day after day after day. Alejandro agreed.

He wasn't sure which of those four had come up with the idea for his football pants. His parents were the ones who explained the idea to him. He told them that, sorry, he couldn't play anymore because his pants had been cut up at the hospital. They smiled.

"What a great opportunity to show yourself that you've learned something about real courage," his mom said.

"Speaking of showing things," his dad said, "let me show you how to use our sewing machine. You're going to need it for your pants."

Which is why, today, on the sideline, he kept scratching his leg. Learning how to use the sewing machine hadn't been easy, but eventually he had gotten the hang of it. Still, the thread itched a little—especially when he had nothing to do. No one to talk to and no hope of getting on the field.

Or at least he thought there was no way of getting in the game—until the whistles blew and Coach Drummer went speed walking onto the field.

Grant, the backup running back who was now their starting running back, was lying on the field.

"You okay, Melvin?" Coach asked him. Then he asked him how many fingers he was holding up.

DeSean couldn't hear Grant's answer, but Coach

was concerned enough to send his starting running back to the sideline.

"Mitchell, you're in," Coach yelled.

And just like that, DeSean forgot all about his itchy leg.

He passed Grant who, no kidding, was smiling as he limped off the field. DeSean wondered briefly if Grant had faked an injury just like DeSean had. But if he had, DeSean didn't blame him. In a few moments, both would be where they wanted to be. Grant would be off the field. DeSean would be in the huddle.

He didn't even care that all his teammates were glaring at him. He was too excited to get a chance to run away from the competition.

Nick called a dive play—a handoff up the gut.

Once everyone was lined up, Nick called, "Hut!" He took the snap and gave the ball to DeSean.

And DeSean saw he had nowhere to go.

The Park City defense smashed him into the field. As he lay there, waiting for the Park City players to get up so he could too, the thought occurred to him that maybe his teammates had let him get smashed. They were planning to take matters into their own hands against Jimmy. Maybe they were doing the same to him now?

And if they were taking matters into their own hands, that was okay too. He was just going to keep getting up. Getting up was what took real courage.

Besides, even if his teammates weren't blocking for him, he wasn't so easy to tackle. To keep DeSean from breaking free took a lot of players and some luck.

Their luck ran out in the second half. DeSean broke through the line. He stutter stepped inside, then bounced outside toward the sideline. Switching the ball from his left arm to his right, he turned on the jets. He could see the end zone in front of him, still half a field away but getting closer with every stride.

Forty yards away.

Thirty.

No high-stepping, he reminded himself. *No fumbling.*

He crossed the fifteen-yard line.

And turned his head to make sure he was in the clear.

He wasn't.

A Park City player launched at him. The player's shoulder drove into his hip. The player's arms wrapped around his waist.

Then the player laughed.

"Jimmy?" DeSean said.

"That's me." Jimmy let out a laugh.

"Why are you laughing?" DeSean asked.

"Why are you?" Jimmy replied.

Jimmy was right. DeSean, without even realizing it, was lying there on the field, laughing like a crazy person.

"I forgot about how much fun this can be," DeSean said. "I can't believe I almost gave all this up."

"Exactly what I was thinking," said Jimmy.

The two players helped each other up.

"See you at the goal line?" DeSean asked.

"I'll be there." Jimmy grinned.

DeSean sprinted back to his huddle. He didn't need to hurry. There was plenty of time on the clock. He just felt like running.

ABOUT the AUTHOR

Paul Hoblin is the author of several sports novels, including *Foul*, a basketball-horror story that *Booklist* called "unbearably tense." Under a different name (Patrick Hueller), his latest book is *Read at Your Own Peril*, a novel in which all reading has been banned because it puts kids in comas. One teenage reader described the book as "thrilling, powerful, eye-opening . . . a book totally worth risking your life for!"

GLOSSARY

ACL (AYE SEE ELL)—short for "anterior cruciate ligament," one of the major ligaments in the knee

archrival (ARCH-RYE-vuhl)—a team's biggest rival

clutch (KLUHCH)—referring to the end of the game when there is more pressure

linebacker (LYNE-bak-er)—a defensive football player who lines up immediately behind the line of scrimmage to make tackles on running plays or defend against short passes

MCL (EMM SEE ELL)—short for "medial collateral ligament," a band of tissue on the inside of the knee

nimble (NIM-buhl)—movement that is light and quick

pylon (PYE-lon)—a small, orange marker placed at each of the corners of the end zone of a football field

running back (RUH-ning BAK)—an offensive football player whose main role is to move the ball toward the end zone by running with it

squib (SKWIB)—kicking the football low and short so it bounces across the field before someone catches it

up the gut (UHP THUH GUHT)—a football play in which the player runs the ball through the middle of the field through defenders

DISCUSSION QUESTIONS

1. Do you understand why DeSean pretended to be injured? Is he a bad person for doing this? Is there a difference between making a bad decision and being a bad person? Give an example.

2. Royce says it doesn't matter whether Jimmy was trying to hurt DeSean; what matters is that the tackle was dangerous, so he should be suspended for it. Do you agree or disagree? Why?

3. Is Alejandro being a good friend or disloyal when he finds Jimmy and brings him to see DeSean? Explain your answer.

WRITING PROMPTS

1. Write about a time when you were really embarrassed in public. Describe the situation. Where were you? Use your senses. What could you see, hear, smell? How did you feel physically? What made the situation so embarrassing?

2. Pretend you are one of DeSean's teammates. Describe watching him return the kickoff for what you think is going to be a game-winning touchdown. Then he drops the ball before scoring. What are your thoughts? How do you feel?

3. Jimmy apologizes to DeSean. Why does Jimmy feel the need to apologize? Do you think he did anything wrong?

MORE ABOUT FOOTBALL BLOOPERS

DeSean is a fictional middle school football player. But there are many real pro and college football players who have dropped the ball at the one-yard line, including one named DeSean!

- In a 2008 game against the Dallas Cowboys, star Philadelphia Eagles wide receiver DeSean Jackson dropped the ball inches before crossing the goal line. Luckily for him, the Eagles kept the ball and scored on the next play.

- A few years later, Denver Broncos cornerback Danny Trevathan intercepted a pass and ran it back for a touchdown. Well, almost. He dropped the ball at the one-yard line. The ball kept rolling through and out of the end zone for a touchback.

- During the 2014–15 college football season, Oregon Duck player Byron Marshall fumbled the ball just before scoring. Then, later in the season, he did it again.

- In 2016, Clemson punt returner Ray-Ray McCloud zigged and zagged from one end of the field to the other. In the process, his shoe fell off. It was an amazing return. Or it would have been, if he hadn't dropped the ball too early. The other team recovered the fumble.

- In 2014, Utah wide receiver Kaelin Clay caught a deep pass and raced away from his defenders. Like all the others on this list, though, he forgot to do one thing: hold on to the ball until he crossed the goal line. While Clay and his teammates celebrated what they thought was a touchdown, the other team, the Oregon Ducks, picked up the football and ran it 100 yards for the touchdown.

Believe it or not, there are several more pro and college players who have made the same mistake. You can find videos and articles about these players on the internet. It really is true that everyone, even incredible athletes, make mistakes.